Items should be returned on or before the last date shown below. Items not already requested by other borrowers may be renewed in person, in writing or by telephone. To renew, please quote the number on the barcode label. To renew online a PIN is required. This can be requested at your local library.
Renew online @ **www.dublincitypubliclibraries.ie**
Fines charged for overdue items will include postage incurred in recovery. Damage to or loss of items will be charged to the borrower.

Leabharlanna Poiblí Chathair Bhaile Átha Cliath
Dublin City Public Libraries

Date Due	Date Due	Date Due
0 5 FEB 2019		

D1422068

Twink

Bimi

Pix

Sooze

Sili

Zena

Mariella

Lola

FAIRY SCHOOL

Book Two

Midnight Feast

TITANIA WOODS

Illustrated by Smiljana Coh

BLOOMSBURY

LONDON BERLIN NEW YORK SYDNEY

Bloomsbury Publishing, London, Berlin, New York and Sydney

First published in Great Britain in April 2008 by Bloomsbury Publishing Plc
36 Soho Square, London, W1D 3QY

This paperback edition published in July 2011

A CIP catalogue record for this book is available from the British Library

ISBN 978 1 4088 2021 6

FSC
www.fsc.org

MIX
Paper from
responsible sources
FSC® C018072

Typeset by Dorchester Typesetting Group Ltd
Printed in Great Britain by Clays Ltd, St Ives Plc, Bungay, Suffolk

1 3 5 7 9 10 8 6 4 2

www.fairyschoolbooks.co.uk

For my mother, with love

Chapter One

'Look!' cried Teena. She stood up in her stirrups, pointing eagerly as Glitterwings Academy came into view. 'There it is! I see it!'

Flying up above with her parents, Twink Flutterby looked down at her little sister and smiled. *That was me last term*, she thought. *Riding on a mouse because I couldn't fly yet, and so excited to be seeing Glitterwings!*

Twink's mother stopped and hovered, her eyes shining. 'Oh, isn't it lovely! When I was a student here, I always thought Glitterwings was at its very prettiest in the summer term.'

'You used to say that *every* term, if I recall!' teased Twink's father. His dark purple hair fell over his forehead as he grinned at his wife.

Privately, Twink thought her mother was right. The great oak tree that housed Glitterwings Academy was in full leaf, its strong branches basking in the sun. The tiny windows that wound up its trunk sparkled like dewdrops, and the grand double doors at its base seemed to gleam.

'Come on,' said Twink's father, glancing at the sun. 'We still have quite a way to go after we drop Twink off, if we're to get to Mother's before dinner.'

Twink's spirits plummeted at his words. She had been trying not to think about her family going to Gran's without her, but now she couldn't avoid it. She trailed along after her parents as they skimmed over the bright field of wildflowers that encircled the school.

As they landed, Twink saw crowds of excited fairies flitting about Glitterwings like humming-birds, shouting welcomes to each other. No one

Glitterwings Academy

from Daffodil Branch seemed to be there yet, though, and for a moment Twink felt very alone.

'We'll send you a butterfly when we get to Gran's,' Twink's mother said. She gave Twink a tight hug, her wings folding warmly around her. 'Have a wonderful birthday, darling. I'm sorry we can't be with you on the day, but I'm sure you'll have a good time with your friends.'

Twink forced a smile. 'Oh, it'll be glimmery! I can hardly wait.'

'That's the spirit, Twinkster.' Her father hugged

her, too, and Twink knew that she hadn't fooled him. He handed her her oak-leaf bag and ruffled her bright pink hair. 'Have a good term, love. We'll see you soon.'

Twink waved as hard as she could as her family departed. Teena twisted about in Brownie's stirrups, shouting goodbyes until they had all disappeared from view.

Twink's hand dropped to her side. Her bright lavender wings drooped. That was that, then. Her family was gone.

'Twink!' cried a voice.

Twink spun quickly about, and saw her best friend. 'Bimi!' The two girls embraced, lifting off the grass as their wings fluttered excitedly.

'Isn't it great to be back?' laughed Bimi. 'I never thought I'd miss this place when I first came here, but I really did – everything at home just seemed boring!'

Twink's smile slipped away. She dropped back to the ground with a *thump*. 'Yes, I – I suppose so,' she said.

Bimi landed beside her, staring. 'You *suppose* so? Twink, what's wrong?'

'Oh, nothing.' All at once tears threatened. Twink made a face, trying desperately not to cry. She didn't want to say what was wrong – she knew how stupid and babyish it would sound.

Bimi's eyes were full of concern. She drew Twink quickly away behind a cluster of bluebells. The fragrant blossoms cast soft shadows over the grass, shielding the two girls from prying eyes.

'Twink, you have to tell me!' insisted Bimi. 'What is it?'

Twink wiped her eyes. 'It's – it's my birthday on Friday.'

Bimi looked confused. 'What's so bad about that?'

Twink felt a lump in her throat. She took a deep breath. 'It's just – well, my family always make it a really special day for me. We go to my grand-mother's, and – and it's always just wonderful.' She bit her lip, thinking of Gran's cosy kitchen and delicious honey cakes.

'Oh, Twink.' Bimi touched her arm.

'But this year I'll be at school for my birthday,' continued Twink. 'And Gran was away during the hols, so I didn't get to see her. She's only just got back, and now my family's going to go and see her without me. They'll be doing all these glimmery things without me on my birthday – it's like they don't even care!'

Bimi rubbed her silver and gold wing against Twink's lavender one. 'Twink, I'm sure they care! But it's really too bad that you have to miss all the fun.'

Twink swallowed hard, already ashamed of her outburst. She knew that her parents had tried their best to make it up to her, with a special party at home before she left. It wasn't their fault that her gran had been away, or that Twink's birthday fell during Glitterwings term-time.

'I've just – I've just never had a birthday without them before,' she said softly. Her cheeks reddened as she looked down. 'It's going to feel a bit strange, that's all.'

Bimi nodded sympathetically. 'I know. I'm glad

my birthday comes in the holidays. But you know, *that* will be strange, too, not being able to spend it with my friends from school.'

Twink hadn't thought of that. She stroked a bluebell's smooth leaf. 'I suppose things are different when you go away to school, aren't they? We're not babies any more, and things are just harder sometimes.'

'That's true,' said Bimi. 'But they're better, too. Look at us – we can fly now, and we're going to the best school in the world!'

They smiled at each other. Twink thought how glad she was that she could talk to someone this way. She was the luckiest fairy in the school, to have Bimi for a best friend.

'Come on,' she said suddenly. 'Let's go to Daffy Branch, and make sure we've got beds beside each other again!'

The two girls took off, swooping over grass and flowers. Twink laughed as they zoomed through the double doors of the school at full speed, dodging fairies from older years.

'Watch it, you kids!' someone shouted after them.

When they got inside, Twink paused, gazing upwards. The inside of Glitterwings was even more wonderful than the outside: a high, high tower filled with a soft golden light. Fairies flitted in and out of its many branches like brightly coloured birds.

'Hurry!' said Bimi. The swirling gold and silver pattern of Bimi's wings sparkled as she took off, and Twink remembered how she had thought Bimi the most beautiful fairy she had ever seen when she first met her. Now she was simply Bimi – her friend.

She flew to catch up with Bimi and the two fairies spiralled upwards, passing empty classrooms and dorm branches filled with arriving fairies. On impulse, Twink did a quick somersault in the air, the wind tickling her wings.

Bimi laughed. Twink grinned back at her, feeling a bit better. It had taken her ages to learn to fly the term before – much to her embarrassment when the rest of the first year was whizzing about like dragonflies! Now, though, she couldn't get enough of it.

It'll be all right, she told herself firmly. *I learned how to fly, so I can learn anything – even how to be away from my family on my birthday.*

When the girls reached Daffodil Branch, Twink saw with satisfaction that it was just as they had left it – a snug, comfortable branch with cosy moss beds and glow-worm lamps. An upside-down daffodil hung over each bed like a canopy. Their uniforms would be daffodils, too, with the jaunty oak-leaf cap that every student at Glitterwings wore.

'Look, we can have the same beds as last time!' cried Bimi. She and Twink flitted quickly to the two beds nearest the window. 'Oh, good!' said Bimi, bouncing on hers. 'I was worried that we wouldn't be together.'

A few of the other girls had already arrived and were putting away their things. Pix, a clever red-headed fairy, grinned and flapped her yellow wings. 'We saved them for you!' she called.

'Thanks!' Twink called back with a smile.

A fairy with a pointed face and silvery-green hair sniffed loudly. 'Well, *I* don't think it's fair, saving beds for people! Maybe Lola and I would have liked to sleep there.'

Twink made a face at her, and didn't answer. 'Mariella hasn't got any nicer, I see,' she muttered to Bimi.

'No, she's still her same old wonderful self,' agreed Bimi. 'Lucky us!'

Twink opened up her oak-leaf bag and began to unpack. Carefully, she arranged her things on the soft brown surface of her bedside mushroom: her thistle comb, a bottle of sparkly wing polish, the drawings of her family.

Their faces smiled out at her. Twink sighed, her fingers lingering on the drawings. It was very odd, imagining them all at Gran's house without her.

'It'll be all right, Twink, really!' whispered Bimi.

Twink managed a smile. 'I'm OK,' she said. Suddenly she caught sight of something crouching on Bimi's bedside mushroom, and her eyes widened. 'Bimi! You've got a cricket clock!'

Bimi nodded, patting the insect on his shiny brown head. He waved his antennae with a cheerful chirp. 'Yes, my dad got him for me. He knows what a hard time I have waking up in the morning!'

'How does it work?' Twink tickled the cricket under his chin.

Bimi showed her a small petal pad. 'You just write down the time you want waking up, and tuck it under his front foot. They forget otherwise – crickets love to help, but they don't have very good memories!'

Before Twink could reply, a shout rang through the branch. 'Opposite! There you are!'

Sooze! Twink whirled about as an energetic fairy

zoomed into the branch, almost knocking her over with an enthusiastic hug.

'Hurrah, my Opposite is here!' said Sooze, flapping her wings. 'Isn't it glimmery to be back?'

Twink grinned. Sooze always called her 'Opposite', because where Twink had bright pink hair and lavender wings, Sooze had lavender hair and pink wings. The two girls had been best friends for much of the last term, and Twink still liked Sooze – even though she'd found out that she wasn't the most dependable fairy in the world!

'It's great,' Twink agreed happily, tucking a strand of pink hair behind her ear. 'Did you have good hols, Sooze?'

Bimi's expression had turned stiff the moment Sooze flitted into the branch. She fed her cricket a leaf without saying anything.

'Glimmery!' Sooze threw herself on to Twink's bed and bounced up and down. 'My sister Winn and I did loads of things. Oh, and, Twink, she has all *sorts* of ideas for things we First Years can do to liven things up around here! We're really falling behind compared to what she got up to last term.'

'What's wrong with things the way they are?' asked Bimi coolly. Twink winced. She knew that Bimi didn't like Sooze very much.

Sooze rolled her eyes. 'Well, we only played *one* good prank on Madame last term! And we didn't do anything *really* fun. We've got a lot of catching-up to do, I can tell you!'

Twink saw Bimi's lips tighten. 'Have we got our new timetables yet?' she asked quickly. 'We're supposed to start Creature Kindness this term – I can hardly wait! What about you two?'

She looked hopefully at them both. If she could just get them chatting about something, maybe the three of them could all get on and be friends.

But Bimi didn't say anything, and Sooze just laughed, fluttering her pink wings. 'That's all we need, another class! But Winn says Mr Woodleaf is a real pushover. We should have lots of fun with *him*.'

Twink laughed too, but was relieved when Mrs Hover, the matron, arrived just then. The silver-winged fairy huffed a bit as her ample frame touched down on the ledge outside the branch.

'Hoo!' she gasped, fanning herself with her wings. 'That flight gets steeper every time I do it. Hello, girls – are we all here?' She counted them quickly, and nodded with satisfaction. 'Excellent! Come along, now – it's time for the opening gathering in the Great Branch.'

The first gathering of the new term! Twink's wings tingled with excitement. She skimmed across the branch and took off into the trunk with the others. They streamed downwards, single-file. The air hummed with hundreds of wings as fairies from other years and branches appeared, shouting happily to each other.

As they all poured into the Great Branch, Twink saw their table near the front: a long mossy table with a large yellow daffodil suspended over it. Different flowers and plants hung over the other tables, and glow-worm lanterns hung from the ceiling. When it was dark, they lit the Branch like pieces of sunshine.

'Come on!' cried Twink to Bimi, rushing to their table. The two friends grinned at each other as they grabbed seats side by side on the red and white spotted mushrooms. On the platform above them, the Glitterwings teachers sat talking.

Twink saw Mrs Lightwing, their Flight mistress and first-year head, and bit back a rueful smile. The gruff, no-nonsense teacher hadn't had an easy time of it last term, trying to teach Twink how to fly!

Once the fairies were all seated, Miss Shimmery, the HeadFairy, hovered into the air and clapped her hands for attention. Silence fell over the Great Branch. There was a rustling noise as the students all twisted on their mushrooms to face her, their expressions expectant.

'A warm welcome to all of our students,' said Miss Shimmery in her low voice. Her white hair shone, and her rainbow wings glimmered gracefully. 'It's a new term, and I expect a lot of good work from all of you. In fact, I expect much better work than last term, when a few of you took the *fairy fun* in our school song a bit too much to heart!'

Her gaze fell on a fourth-year table halfway along the Branch. Looking over her shoulder, Twink saw the Primrose table – the branch where Sooze's sister Winn lived. Winn and her friends grinned sheepishly at each other.

'Now, I know that *some* pranks are inevitable in a school full of young fairies, but there will be far less this term,' said Miss Shimmery firmly. 'If anyone finds it difficult to settle down, we'll assume that you have too much free time, and need more to do. Does everyone understand?'

The Branch was so silent that you could have heard a mouse sniff. Miss Shimmery scanned the school. A very slight twinkle shone in her eyes, but Twink knew that she meant exactly what she said.

'I'm glad that we understand each other,' smiled Miss Shimmery at last. 'Now then – all rise, and sing the Glitterwings song!'

Twink stood up with the others. The school cricket-band jumped into place behind Miss Shimmery, and a moment later their rousing music filled the Branch. The fairies eagerly lifted their voices, opening and closing their wings in time to the song.

> *Oh, Glitterwings, dear Glitterwings*
> *Beloved oak tree scho-ool.*
> *Good fairy fun for everyone,*
> *That is our fairy ru-ule.*
> *Our teachers wise,*
> *Their magic strong,*
> *With all our friends,*
> *We can't go wrong.*
> *Oh, Glitterwings, dear Glitterwings*
> *Beloved oak tree scho-ool.*

'Butterflies commence!' announced Miss Shimmery as the song ended. She lifted her arm and a colourful stream of butterflies swept into the Branch, carrying oak-leaf platters piled high with seed cakes and acorn jugs of fresh dew. The tables buzzed into conversation as the girls sat down and started to eat.

'It sounds like a challenge to me!' grinned Sooze,

sprinkling pollen over her cake. 'How much can we get away with without being caught?'

Pix shook her bright head. 'I think we'd better be careful. Miss Shimmery wasn't joking.'

Twink played with her food as the conversation went on around her. Her family had probably arrived at Gran's house by now. Gran lived in a snug tree stump in a green wood, and her home was always bright and clean, with delicious smells drifting from it. A neighbouring mole family lived nearby, and Twink and Teena always had great fun playing with the babies. And at night, Gran would tell wonderful stories about life when she was a young fairy.

All of that would be going on without her now, thought Twink. Would her family even remember her on her birthday? *Oh, don't be silly!* she scolded herself. Of course they would.

'Are you all right?' whispered Bimi.

Twink smiled gratefully at her friend. 'I'm fine,' she said. She took a bite of seed cake and sighed, thinking of the wonderful honey cake that Gran always made for her birthday.

'I'm fine,' she repeated. 'But . . . I'll be a lot happier once my birthday is over with.'

Chapter Two

Long after the others had gone to sleep that night, Bimi lay awake in her bed beside the window, worrying about her friend. Poor Twink! What an awful thing, to feel so alone on your birthday. What could she do to cheer her up?

I'll give her my new snail-trail pen for a present, she decided. Her mother had bought it for her during the holiday. It was the very latest thing – a pen that left a sparkly silver snail-trail. Twink would love it, Bimi knew.

All right, a present was good . . . but she wanted

to do something really special for Twink, too. Bimi frowned, staring up at the moonlit ceiling. A party? Yes, but not just any party. It had to be super-glimmery, so that Twink would forget that her family was at Gran's without her.

But all Bimi could think of was having a party in the Common Branch. Boring! *Oh, why aren't I clever like Pix*, she thought in despair. *I want to surprise Twink somehow!*

She gasped suddenly. Of course, that was it – they'd throw a surprise party for Twink! Even better, they could have a midnight feast. What a glimmery idea! Even the Common Branch would seem special and exciting at midnight.

Miss Shimmery's warning floated into Bimi's mind, and she frowned worriedly. Secret midnight feasts probably weren't what the HeadFairy had in mind when she had told them all to work hard and settle down!

I'll need help planning it so that we don't get caught, thought Bimi. She'd get Pix on her own tomorrow, and see if the clever fairy had any ideas. Bimi had hardly ever broken a rule in her life . . . but this was important. A midnight feast might be the only thing that would cheer up her friend.

Bimi smiled as she drifted off to sleep, imagining the look of delight on Twink's face when she found out. Her best friend was going to have the most glimmery birthday party ever!

'Chirp-chirp! Chirp-chirp!'

Twink's eyes flickered open as Bimi's cricket clock went off. Drowsily, she sat up and watched Bimi pat the creature on the head. He fell silent.

'Thanks, cricket,' said Bimi.

'He works!' said Twink.

Bimi grinned. 'Well, of course he works. Isn't he great?' She jumped out of bed. Humming to herself, she picked up her thistle comb and brushed her dark blue hair.

Twink's eyes widened. Bimi was never in such a cheerful mood so early in the day, but she seemed very pleased with herself this morning.

Before she could ask Bimi what she was so happy

23

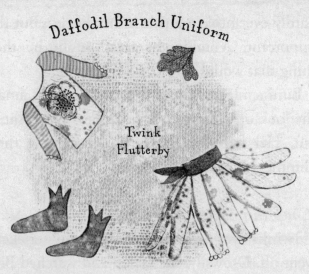

Daffodil Branch Uniform

Twink
Flutterby

about, Mrs Hover bustled into the branch, her arms
full of yellow and white daffodils. 'Wake up, sleepy-
heads! Rise and shine, my loves!'

Our new uniforms! thought Twink, bouncing out
of bed herself.

In no time at all, Mrs Hover had fitted them with
their new school dresses – a pinch of pink and gold
fairy dust from the pouch at her hip, and the
flowers instantly became dresses in each girl's size.
Glimmery! Twink twirled in her new white flower-
dress, admiring its yellow trim.

'When can we make our dresses ourselves?' called Sooze from across the branch. She adjusted her oak-leaf cap at a rakish angle.

Tutting loudly, Mrs Hover padded across and tugged her cap firmly straight. 'Not until fifth year. You have to have a good few years of Fairy Dust class before you can transform things properly!'

'Do the upper years all make theirs?' asked Pix. Her daffodil dress was bright yellow, to match her yellow wings.

Mrs Hover nodded grimly. 'Yes, and I have to watch them like a cat. They'd fair make your wings curl, the things they try to get away with with those dresses! Now, who wants a timetable?'

Twink crowded around with the others as Mrs Hover passed out the rose-petal timetables with their names written on them. 'Look, we *do* start Creature Kindness this term,' she said, nudging Bimi with her wing. 'I can hardly wait!'

'Oh, not Double Flight first thing!' moaned Mariella, scowling down at her petal. 'Doesn't Mrs

Lightwing think we know how to fly yet?' She stopped, smirking at Twink. 'Of course, some of us who were *slow starters* may not have quite mastered it . . .'

She poked her friend Lola, a thin, pale fairy with washed-out blue wings. The two of them snickered as Twink's face reddened.

Bimi glared at Mariella. 'Just remind me, who won the award for best flier last term?' she asked pointedly.

Mariella's face darkened as the rest of the Branch laughed. She had been furious when Twink, and not herself, had won the award. Twink gave Bimi a grateful grin.

'Now now, none of that!' said Mrs Hover briskly, shepherding them towards the ledge. 'Come on, everyone – time for breakfast.'

'Right!' said Mrs Lightwing, hovering above the First Years. Her sky-blue hair was pulled back into a stern bun. 'We're going to work on barrel rolls today. I'm tired of seeing sloppy wingwork when you come out of the roll.'

Twink listened carefully. She knew that most of the other First Years were impatient with Flight class by now, but she herself had only learned to fly at the end of last term. Finally, she'd get to have some fun in this class!

Mrs Lightwing flitted back and forth in front of the long line of fairies. 'Barrel rolls aren't just done for a laugh, you know! They can be a vital manoeuvre for getting out of a tight spot.' On the other side of the flying field, Glitterwings rose up towards the sky, its windows glinting in the sunshine.

'Now, let's do some practice.' Mrs Lightwing tapped her wings together. 'Twink, you and Pix fly together this term. Everyone else, please get in the same teams as last term.'

Oh, no! Twink glanced quickly at Bimi. Her best friend looked like she had just been drenched with freezing rain.

'But, Miss –' started Bimi. She stopped abruptly, her face colouring up.

Mrs Lightwing swept over to her, hovering a few inches above the flying field. 'Yes?' she barked.

Bimi looked at Twink, who nodded encouragement at her. *Go on!* she thought fervently.

'Please, Miss, could I be in a different group?' burst out Bimi.

Mrs Lightwing frowned. 'And what's wrong with the group you have?' she demanded.

Twink saw Mariella watching Bimi with narrowed eyes, and shuddered. Poor Bimi! It was bad enough that she had had to fly on Mariella's team all last term. Surely Mrs Lightwing wouldn't make her do it again!

Bimi took a deep breath and straightened her wings. 'I don't want to fly with Mariella,' she said.

The Flight mistress raised a sky-blue eyebrow. 'Oh? And why not?'

Bimi's face was on fire. 'I – I don't like her,' she said.

A snicker ran through the class. Even Lola gave a hysterical giggle, and Twink saw Mariella's face turn purple with anger. 'You just wait!' she hissed at Bimi under her breath.

Mrs Lightwing looked sharply at her. 'Wait for what, Mariella?'

Mariella's scowl deepened. 'Nothing, Miss,' she said sulkily.

'Hmm.' Mrs Lightwing tapped her wings together. 'All right, Bimi, you can fly with Twink and Pix instead. Mariella, you and Lola can fly alone – until you become more pleasant and others want to be around you!'

As Mariella seethed, Twink and Bimi exchanged an excited look and squeezed hands. *Oh, hurrah!* thought Twink. They'd get to fly together – how perfectly glimmery!

Mrs Lightwing blew her reed whistle. 'All right, now, teams in the air. We'll start with a series of six rolls. And remember – tight wingwork, everyone!'

The fairies took off in a flurry, causing a group of nearby midges to dart away in alarm. As Twink, Pix and Bimi searched for an empty space of sky to practise in, Mariella darted up, with Lola hovering close behind.

'How *dare* you show me up in front of the whole year, Bimi?' Mariella's voice trembled with rage. 'You won't get away with it! I'll –'

'Oh, buzz off!' snapped Pix. 'It's not Bimi's fault you're so awful. Everyone in the whole year knows it!'

Mariella clenched her fists as if she might explode. She zoomed off abruptly, glaring at Bimi over her shoulder.

Bimi swallowed hard, looking shaken. 'I think she really hates me now! But I *couldn't* fly with her again, I just couldn't!'

'Of course not!' Twink flew close to Bimi and rubbed her wing against hers. 'Don't worry about Mariella. She's just a wasp brain.'

The girls started on their barrel rolls, first getting up a good head of speed and then tucking their wings in as they twisted in the air. Twink grinned, her pink hair whipping about her face. Barrel rolls were good fun, no matter what Mrs Lightwing said!

As they came out of their last roll, she glanced over at Mariella and shook her head. She had never

seen Mariella quite so angry before. Bimi would probably do well to avoid her for a while!

Bimi had been trying all morning for a chance to talk to Pix alone, with no luck. Then, after Flight class, Twink solved the problem for her.

'Oh, look, there's Sili!' she cried as they drew near the school. 'I'll be right back – I just want to ask her about her hols.' She skimmed away in a bright blur of pink and lavender.

'Pix, I need to talk to you,' said Bimi urgently once Twink was gone.

Pix glanced at her in surprise. 'All right! What's up?'

Quickly, Bimi explained about Twink's birthday, and her idea for a midnight feast. 'But it needs to be really special! And of course we don't want Mariella and Lola to come, so we'll have to keep it a secret from them, somehow.'

Pix's eyes were shining. 'A midnight feast, what a glimmery idea! But you're right, those two can never know about it. They'd be sure to go straight to Mrs

Lightwing to get us into trouble, and you know what Miss Shimmery said.'

Bimi gulped. Stupidly, it hadn't occurred to her that Mariella and Lola might tell on them, but of course Pix was right. Mariella would *love* to get them all into trouble if she could. Especially her, after this morning!

She peered over her shoulder. Mariella and Lola were flying some way behind the others, whispering behind their hands to each other.

'Maybe it's too risky,' said Bimi doubtfully. 'Should we just have an ordinary party at break time?'

Pix shook her head. 'No, we should have a midnight feast for Twink – it's perfect! We won't get caught if we plan it right.'

They flew through the great double doors. 'What about Sooze?' said Pix suddenly. 'I know she's not your favourite fairy, but you should ask her to help you plan, too – she's sure to have loads of great ideas!'

Bimi made a face, but she knew Pix was right.

Sooze was wonderful at this sort of thing. With her help, Twink's party would really be something to remember.

'All right,' she said. 'Let's make some sort of excuse to Twink at break, and the three of us can talk about it then.'

'A midnight feast? Oh, that's perfect!' cried Sooze. 'It's just what we need to liven things up around here!'

The three girls were sitting on mushroom seats in the Glitterwings library – a high ceilinged, narrow room with hundreds of petal-leaf books lining its walls. Overhead, fairies flitted about the shelves like bumblebees, their wings buzzing.

Honestly, thought Bimi. It was just like Sooze to care more about *livening things up* than cheering up their friend!

'Yes, we're having it in the Common Branch on Friday night.' Bimi tried not to let her irritation show. 'So I just wondered if you had any ideas about –' She stopped. Sooze was shaking her lavender head firmly.

'Not the Common Branch!' she said. 'It's too boring! You know where we should have it?' Sooze leaned forward, her eyes sparkling.

'Where?' asked Pix.

'In the Dingly Dell!' said Sooze triumphantly. 'It's this little dell not far from the school – my sister Winn told me all about it. It's supposed to be *so* glimmery. There's a stream, and carpets of flowers, and slides made from reeds – it's a real fairy fun-spot!'

Dingly Dell

Bimi and Pix looked at each other. 'Leave the school?' said Bimi slowly. 'Sooze, I don't know – it seems risky enough just having a party at all.'

Sooze flapped a wing at her. 'Oh, don't be such a wet leaf! It's easy, Winn has done it loads of times. You want to have a really special party for Twink, don't you?'

Bimi's mouth tightened. 'Of course, but –'

'Sooze, are you *sure* it would be safe?' interrupted Pix. 'How would we do it? Don't they lock the doors at night?'

Sooze laughed. 'Who needs doors? We can fly, can't we? We'll just go out of one of the windows! The only thing is, they don't open from the outside, so someone will need to stay behind to let us back in again. Or else two fairies could take turns, so they each get to go to half the party.'

Bimi bit her lip. Her simple little party suddenly seemed to have become very complex and dangerous!

But Pix didn't seem to think so. She nodded thoughtfully. 'You know, we're actually *less* likely to get caught if we're not in the school. I think that could really work, Sooze!'

'Of course it will!' Sooze flipped back her lavender hair. 'I told you, Winn's done it loads of times. And she says the Dingly Dell is *so* worth it – it's just the most magical place ever!'

'What about food?' Pix took a leaf-pad out of her bag and started to write. 'We'll need lots of it!'

Sooze grinned. 'Well, it's lucky that it's the start of term – everyone's brought goodies from home that we can share. Plus Winn says that –'

Bimi's wings felt stiff as the two of them excitedly carried on swapping ideas. Already the party felt as though it didn't belong to her any more. Sooze had taken it over.

I'm being silly, she told herself. *The important thing is that Twink has a good time. Besides, she'll know it was my idea!*

Chapter
Three

In the days that followed, Twink became certain that the fairies in her branch were up to something. They were always whispering together – and when Twink asked what they were talking about, they'd insist that it was nothing at all. Even Bimi was acting strangely! Twink's best friend seemed to have something on her mind, and had gone very quiet lately.

Things came to a head after dinner on Thursday night, when Twink flew into the first-year Common Branch. Madame Brightfoot had taught them some glimmery new dance moves that afternoon, and Twink was anxious to try them out with the others. And it was the perfect time – she had just seen Mariella and Lola heading for the library. The Common Branch without those two sitting sneering in the corner was something to be savoured!

She flitted into the room and stopped short. The Daffy Branch fairies were all huddled together, and seemed to be softly arguing about something. Only Bimi, who stood off to one side with a pained expression on her face, kept silent as their whispered voices grew louder.

Her pointed ears burning with curiosity, Twink edged forward until she could hear them.

'Well, it can't be me!' said Sooze. 'I'm the only one who knows the way, so I *can't* stay behind.'

'Oh, you just don't want to miss any of the party!' laughed Zena. 'The place can't be *that* hard to get to, if your wasp brain sister managed it.'

Sooze gave her a mock scowl, but Pix interrupted before she could reply. 'We'll have to cast pebbles. *None* of us wants to miss any of the party, so it's only fair.'

Party? Twink stood rooted to the spot, wings frozen. 'What are you talking about?' she burst out.

Suddenly the Daffy Branch fairies all looked as if they had swallowed ladybirds! 'Oh, Twink, you weren't meant to hear!' wailed Sili.

Twink put her hands on her hips. 'But I *did* hear! What are you up to? What party?'

Sooze grinned suddenly. 'We might as well tell you in that case! Twink, we –'

'No!' cried Bimi, flapping her wings. 'It's meant to be a surprise!'

Twink looked at her friend in astonishment. Bimi had been so quiet lately, but suddenly she almost looked like she was going to cry.

Sooze rolled her eyes. 'Oh, the surprise is already ruined, so why not!' She flitted over and squeezed Twink's hand. 'Listen, Opposite – we're all going to have a midnight feast for your birthday tomorrow night. Well, except for Mariella and her little mosquito friend, of course!'

Zena

Good-natured grumbles came from the other fairies. 'Oh, trust Sooze not to keep a secret!' scoffed Pix. 'Twink, we meant to *surprise* you!'

'A midnight feast?' gasped Twink. 'Really?'

'Even better than that!' said Zena. She leaned forward and whispered, 'Sooze has had the best idea – we're going to have it at the Dingly Dell!'

Pix nodded. 'She's thought of everything. It's going to be the best party ever, Twink.'

Twink's wings tickled with excitement. The Dingly Dell! She had heard all about it from Sooze

– it sounded like the most wonderful, magical spot in the world.

'Oh, how glimmery!' she breathed. 'Sooze, thank you!'

She saw Bimi's face fall, and groaned to herself. Oh, no – she might have known that Bimi would be jealous of anything to do with Sooze!

'Thank *all* of you,' she added hastily, looking at Bimi. 'I can hardly wait for tomorrow night.'

'Well, anything to cheer you up!' said Sooze. The others laughed, jostling Twink with their wings and making teasing comments – but Bimi just made a sour face and turned away.

Twink stared after her, hurt. What was wrong with her? Didn't she want Twink to have a party?

Sooze hooked an arm through Twink's. 'Come on, Opposite – I'll show you all the food for tomorrow night. Winn told me about a loose knothole, and we've been hiding everything there!'

Still stung over Bimi's reaction, Twink allowed herself to be lead away. At least you never had to worry about Sooze being in a funny mood! The

lavender-haired fairy was always bright and fun.

The next day Twink could hardly concentrate on her lessons. Madame Brightfoot sighed loudly at her fumbling of dance moves, and Miss Petal, their Flower Power teacher, stopped her demonstration on how to heal buttercups.

'Twink Flutterby, have you been listening to a word I've said?' demanded the pretty young teacher.

Twink started. She had been gazing out of the window, dreaming of the Dingly Dell. 'Oh – yes, Miss!' she said hastily.

Miss Petal smiled sweetly at her. 'Good. Then perhaps you'd like to come and demonstrate how to help this poorly buttercup.'

Oh, wasps! Twink glanced at Bimi for help, but her friend just shrugged and looked away.

Twink's stomach tightened. Bimi had hardly said a word to her since the night before.

'*Now,* Twink – not next solstice,' said Miss Petal.

Someone snickered. Mariella, of course! Reluctantly, Twink rose from her mushroom seat

and fluttered to the front of the branch.

The buttercup sat in a walnut-shell pot, its leaves and petals drooping pitifully. Remembering her Flower Power lessons from last term, Twink put her hands on the flower's leaves. Closing her eyes, she sent the buttercup happy thoughts as hard as she could.

My birthday's today. My friends are having a midnight feast for me, and we're going to the Dingly Dell! Smiling, Twink opened her eyes – and then gasped in dismay. The flower hadn't changed at all!

'You *weren't* listening,' chided Miss Petal. She tapped her yellow wings together. 'I was just saying that buttercups are very relaxed flowers. Happy thoughts don't invigorate them – they need *rousing* thoughts. Going for a mile-long flight, that sort of thing!'

Twink nodded, red-faced. 'Sorry, Miss. I–I was thinking of something else.'

'Ooh, I wonder what?' whispered Sooze loudly. A giggle ran through the class. Twink grinned despite herself at the look of cross confusion on

Mariella's face.

'That's enough, girls!' said Miss Petal. 'You can sit down now, Twink.'

When Twink took her seat again, Bimi was gazing out of the window, ignoring her. Twink's heart sank.

'Bimi, what's wrong?' she murmured as Miss Petal put the buttercup away.

One of Bimi's wings lifted coldly. 'Why don't you ask *Sooze*?' she muttered back.

Oh! Twink let out an angry breath. She knew Bimi was hurt that she was being friendly with Sooze, but it was so unfair! Sooze was planning a party for her – *of course* Twink was going to be friendly to her. And why couldn't she have two friends, anyway?

Scowling down at her petal book, she didn't look at Bimi again for the rest of the lesson.

At dinner that night, Twink and Bimi sat apart for the first time since the new term had begun. Telling herself that she didn't mind, Twink made a point of laughing and talking with the others.

Sooze nudged her with a wing. 'Don't eat too much, Opposite! You want to save your appetite.'

'Save it for what?' asked Mariella, drawing her eyebrows together.

'Oh, I heard there's going to be an extra-special breakfast tomorrow,' said Sooze seriously. 'We want to save some room for it!' Somehow everyone managed to keep a straight face.

Just then the school butterflies streamed into the Great Branch, their jewel-coloured wings glinting brightly. Some of them swooped down over the tables, clearing up dishes and crumbs, while others delivered letters to the fairies.

'Oh!' cried Twink as three butterflies fluttered in front of her, struggling with a large leaf-wrapped package held between them. *Twink Flutterby, Glitterwings Academy*, said the label in her mother's handwriting.

'It's a package from my family, for my birthday!' exclaimed Twink as the tired butterflies dropped the parcel in front of her and flew away.

'Glimmery!' Sooze flapped her wings. 'Open it

now!' Everyone at the table leaned forward, craning to see.

Twink glanced at Bimi. On impulse, she said, 'Bimi, would you help me open it?'

Bimi looked startled, and then slowly smiled. 'All right!'

Twink let out a relieved breath as her friend helped her to untie the strings of plaited grass. Maybe everything would be all right between them after all.

The oak-leaf wrapping fell away, and a gleaming walnut chest sat on the table. Twink creaked open the lid and yelped. 'Look, everyone! It's chock-full of food that my gran made! There's dandelion juice, and sweet seeds – and look, a giant honey cake with my name on it! It's just perfect for tonight!'

'Perfect for tonight?' said Pix. 'What do you mean?' The clever red-haired fairy widened her eyes in warning, motioning towards the end of the table.

Mariella! Twink felt colour sweep her face. How could she have forgotten? 'I – I just meant that I'll share it out in the Common Branch tonight,' she

stammered. 'There's plenty for everyone!'

She looked sideways at Mariella, and was relieved to see her talking to Lola. Phew! Perhaps she hadn't overheard after all. Twink sat down happily, gazing at the chest. Her family hadn't forgotten her. How could she have ever thought they would?

'Oh, I wish I had a pen with me!' she said. 'I could write to my family right now and thank them.'

Sooze lifted her violet eyebrows. 'Well – I was going to save this for later, but –' She reached in her bag and pulled out a present wrapped loosely in a bright pink petal.

'Here you go, Opposite.' She slid it across the table to Twink. 'Many happy returns, and all that!'

Twink tore the wrapping off and gasped in delight. 'A snail-trail pen! Oh, Sooze, thank you! I saw one on my hols, but I didn't have any pocket money left to buy it with!' She uncapped the pen and tested it on her hand, smiling at the sparkly silver ink. 'It's perfect!'

She stretched across the table and hugged Sooze

tightly. Sooze laughed. 'My uncle gave it to me, but I already had one, so I thought of you!'

Bouncing back on to her seat, Twink's smile faded. Bimi was staring at her new pen, her expression stiff and strained.

Oh, not again! thought Twink in exasperation. Wasn't Sooze allowed to do *anything* nice for her?

With dinner finished, the fairies began drifting out of the Great Branch, chattering and laughing. Mariella and Lola were the first to leave the Daffodil Branch table – Mariella with many suspicious frowns.

'Good, they're gone!' said Pix. She glanced at the teachers' platform and lowered her voice. 'We need to finalise our plans for tonight, everyone. We *still* haven't decided who's going to stay behind and open the window.'

Bimi cleared her throat. 'I'll do it.'

Pix grinned. 'Thanks, Bimi, that's really glimmery of you. Now, who else will volunteer, so that Bimi only misses half the party?'

'No, that's not what I meant,' said Bimi in a tight voice. 'I mean I'll just stay behind. Nobody has to miss any of it.'

Twink gaped at her. 'But – but don't you want to go at all?'

Bimi looked away. 'No, I don't feel very well. I'm sort of tired.'

There was a surprised silence. Sooze lifted an eyebrow, looking sceptical. Finally Zena said, 'Well – well, if you're *sure,* Bimi.'

'I'm sure,' said Bimi coolly. 'It's OK, I don't mind.'

'But –' Twink started to protest again and then fell

silent, her lips tightening. Oh, *why* did Bimi have to be like this? She was supposed to be Twink's best friend! She wasn't tired at all – she was just jealous of Twink doing anything with Sooze. She probably wished that Twink wasn't even *having* a party, because Sooze had thought of it and she hadn't!

Twink's wings felt hot. Fine, she decided. If that was the way Bimi wanted to be, it was all right with her!

The plan that night went off perfectly. Just before midnight, Sooze crept about Daffodil Branch, waking up everyone who had fallen asleep.

Twink's eyes flew open when she felt Sooze touch her shoulder. At last, it was time! She climbed quickly out of bed, her wings tingling with excitement. Soft sounds filled the air as everyone got dressed in the moonlight, keeping as silent as they could.

Someone stumbled, bumping against the door. 'Hush!' whispered Sooze. 'Don't wake up Mariella and Lola!'

At that, a loud snore erupted from Mariella's bed. The fairies clutched their mouths to stifle their giggles. 'We'd need an earthquake to wake *her* up!' hissed Sili.

'Come on,' said Pix softly. 'Let's go!'

Twink's heart pounded as they tiptoed across the room. One by one, they flew out into the shadowy, moonlit tree trunk. Twink shivered. Glitterwings at night was very different from the daytime. It seemed larger, somehow, and much more mysterious.

Quickly, they flitted to the secret knothole and passed out food and drink for everyone to carry. 'Here, Twink, you get to carry the cake, because you're the birthday fairy!' grinned Sooze.

Laden down with their goodies, they flew to the window nearest to Daffy Branch. It was just large enough to squeeze through, if they kept their wings tucked in. Twink hung back as Sili, Zena and Pix wormed their way through it, laughing at the tight squeeze.

'Right, now it's our turn!' Sooze's eyes sparkled in the moonlight.

'What time will you be back?' asked Bimi, hovering beside them in her nightdress.

'Three o'clock!' said Sooze. 'We want lots of time to have fun.'

'No, two o'clock,' said Twink. 'That's plenty of time, Sooze – we don't want to get caught.'

Sooze flapped her wings and groaned, but agreed. Bimi crossed her arms over her cobweb dressing gown. 'All right, well – I'll set my cricket clock, and let you back in at two.'

Twink thought her voice sounded forlorn. Suddenly she felt sorry for the angry thoughts she had had earlier, and she squeezed her friend's arm.

'Thanks, Bimi,' she whispered.

'That's all right,' Bimi whispered back. She sounded like she meant it, and Twink's spirits lifted. Oh, it would be so glimmery if things could be all right between them again!

'Come *on*,' said Sooze, fluttering in front of the window. 'This stuff is heavy!'

With a quick goodbye to Bimi, Twink ducked through the window, holding in her wings. A pinch and a pull, and she was out in the moonlight! The others were waiting for her, hovering under the stars.

'At last!' said Pix with a grin. 'All right, everyone, let's get going. To the Dingly Dell!'

Hidden by the shadows, Mariella pressed against the open door of Daffodil Branch. She frowned, straining to hear the whispered conversation taking place across the trunk.

'All right,' she heard Bimi say. 'I'll set my cricket clock, and let you back in at two.'

Mariella smiled smugly. That was all she needed to know!

Silently, she flitted back to her bed and pulled her petal duvet up around her ears. Her silvery-green hair spilled across the pillow as she closed her eyes, pretending to be deeply asleep.

A moment later, she heard Bimi return to the branch and slip back into her own bed. A slight chirrup sounded as she set her clock.

Mariella lay quietly until soft snores came from

Bimi's side of the room. Now! She pushed back her covers and crept to Bimi's bedside. The cricket blinked at her in the moonlight, crouching on Bimi's bedside table. *Two o'clock, and keep very quiet!* was written on a scrap of petal in front of him.

Oh, it was almost too easy! Mariella took the petal and crumpled it up, slipping it into the pocket of her nightdress. Taking another petal from Bimi's bedside drawer, Mariella imitated her looping handwriting. *Seven o'clock,* she wrote.

'She's changed her mind,' she whispered to the cricket, tucking the note under its foot. 'She doesn't want to be woken up until morning.'

The creature looked relieved. Yawning, it tucked its head under its leg.

Mariella returned to bed, smirking broadly. Ha! That would teach Bimi to show her up in front of the whole Flight class! The others would be furious with her now. They'd think she had left them stuck outside on purpose, and would probably never speak to her again.

And better yet, they'd get into trouble, too. Mrs

Lightwing would be livid when she found out about their midnight feast at the Dell. Mariella grinned to herself. It had been a good night's work, all right. She could hardly wait to tell Lola what she had done!

Still smiling, Mariella drifted off to sleep.

Chapter Four

The fairies' wings gleamed in the moonlight as they skimmed lightly over grass and flowers. A warm summer breeze rustled Twink's hair. Up above, the stars glittered like diamonds.

'Oh, this is just glimmery!' breathed Twink, cradling the cake to her chest.

'You haven't seen anything yet!' said Sooze. She led the others down a hill, around a stream, and finally – there it was! The Dingly Dell.

'Oh!' cried all the fairies. It was the most magical little dell imaginable, with a gently tinkling stream, a silvery waterfall and carpets of summer flowers. The moon shone brightly, casting wavering shadows.

'Watch this!' said Sooze with a grin.

Setting her food down on the grass, she flitted towards the stream. A wayward leaf was floating in the water, and Sooze touched down on it lightly. Instantly, it took off into the current. Sooze shrieked with laughter as she rode the leaf through the swiftly moving water, keeping her balance with her wings.

'I want to try that!' cried Twink. She left her food beside Sooze's and grabbed a leaf of her own. It was harder than it looked! She shouted as her leaf spun out into the water, twisting and bucking through the current.

Soon all the fairies were laughing and shrieking, surfing across the water on their leaves. Zena squealed as she tumbled into the stream, and emerged dripping, her yellow hair plastered to her back.

'Oh! It's cold!' she spluttered, laughing.

'Look, there's slides, too!' pointed out Pix. She ran

for the reeds, flitting lightly on top of one. Bouncing to a sitting position, she shot down the reed like a raindrop, tumbling away with a somersault just as she reached the water.

When they grew tired of playing, the fairies stretched out on the grass, bathing their wings in the moonlight. 'Time for food!' said Sili, rubbing her hands together. 'I'm starving.'

Everyone was. Twink parcelled out the goodies, and soon they were all munching happily. 'Twink, your gran makes the best honey cake in the world!' said Sooze, taking another slice. 'This is just glimmery.'

Twink chewed a sweet seed slowly, savouring every bite. It tasted different in the moonlight – sweeter, and even more delicious. Oh, this had to be the best birthday that any fairy had ever had!

But it got even better. When they finished eating, the others gave her their presents. Twink exclaimed with delight as she unwrapped a new bottle of sparkly wing polish from Sili, a woven-grass hair-clip from Pix, and a beautiful rose-petal notebook

from Zena. The notebook was especially fine, with golden flecks of pollen dust glistening across its pages.

'I asked my mother to send it from home,' explained Zena earnestly. 'She makes them herself, and I knew you'd like it.'

'Thank you!' Bouncing to her feet, Twink hugged her friends tightly. 'This has been the best birthday ever. I'll always, always remember it!'

'We'd better get going,' said Pix. She glanced at the moon. 'It's almost two o'clock!'

Sili nodded, fluttering her wings as she stifled a yawn. 'But let's do this again soon! I've had the best time ever.'

The fairies flew back to Glitterwings, tired but happy. The way home seemed much longer, somehow, and Twink gave a contented sigh when she saw the black silhouette of the oak tree rising up against the sky. Soon she'd be snuggled up in her moss bed!

They flew up to the window opposite Daffodil Branch. Twink cupped her hands around the glass

and peered in. The dark school showed no signs of life.

'She's not here yet,' Twink whispered to the others.

The fairies hung in the air, their wings fluttering as they watched the window. The minutes crept by, and still Bimi didn't come. After a while they flew to a nearby branch, resting their tired wings.

'Where *is* she?' wondered Pix, staring worriedly at the window. 'She said she'd be here at two! That's not like Bimi at all.'

Sooze shrugged. 'Maybe she changed her mind.'

'She wouldn't do that!' said Twink fiercely.

Sooze made a face. 'I bet she would! She's been sulking for days about the party.' She dived off the branch. 'Anyway, I'm going to fly around to the Daffy Branch window and look in.'

'Good idea!' said Pix. 'I'll come with you.'

Twink watched as the two of them sped off around the tree. Bimi *wouldn't* just change her mind, not when it was so important. Something must have happened. Maybe Mrs Hover had looked into their branch, and seen them all missing. Twink's wings chilled at the thought. Wasps, they'd *all* be in trouble then.

Soon Sooze and Pix were back, looking grim. Twink bit her lip, already dreading whatever they were going to say.

'Well?' demanded Sili, standing up.

'She's asleep!' announced Sooze. 'Snoring away like anything. We tried knocking on the window, and she just rolled over and ignored us.'

Twink's heart felt like it had fallen to the ground. 'But – but that doesn't make any sense!' she cried. 'Bimi wouldn't just forget about us. She must have set her clock wrong, or something.'

'Ha!' Sooze's face was a thundercloud. 'I bet she never even set it at all. She really doesn't like me, you know. And she hasn't been too happy with *you* lately, either, for being my friend. What a great way to get back at us – just leaving us out here in the dark!'

Twink swallowed. Could Sooze possibly be right? From the expressions on the faces around her, she knew the others thought she could be.

'Well – well, I don't believe it,' she said, clenching her fists. 'She'll be here soon. She has to be! She just set her clock wrong, that's all.'

Sooze smiled, but it wasn't a very pleasant smile. 'Shall we take bets?'

'Come on, there's no point arguing about it.' Pix's face looked worried and pale in the moonlight. 'We've got to find a way in! How about one of the windows in the Great Branch? Maybe one of them is open.'

The fairies flew down the side of the tree, circling about the dark trunk until they reached the Great Branch. Its windows all looked dark . . . and very firmly closed.

'Come on,' whispered Pix. 'I'll start with these windows; the rest of you spread out and start checking some of the others. Even if they look shut, try them anyway! Maybe one of them isn't locked and we can get it open.'

Her heart pounding, Twink flew down the length of the Branch. The huge oak leaves rustled around her as she tried the window nearest her, tugging hard at the wooden frame. Wasps! It didn't budge.

Dodging leaves as she flew, Twink worked her way down the Branch, trying window after window. They were all locked tight! Twink fought back stinging tears. Bimi couldn't really have done this to them, could she? They'd be stuck out here all night!

'Over here!' hissed Sooze's voice from the other side of the Branch. 'I've found one open!'

Twink gasped. Zooming over the top of the Branch, she found Sooze hovering beside an open window. The others arrived from all directions, their faces awash with relief.

'Oh, hurrah!' cried Sili softly. 'We're saved!'

Pix started to say something, but stopped. She usually thought Sili was far too dramatic, but this time Sili wasn't exaggerating!

The fairies squeezed through the window one by one, dropping lightly on to the floor of the Great Branch. Twink shivered as she looked around her. The Branch, so grand and impressive when lit, now looked shadowy and frightening. Oh, wasps, she could hardly wait to get back to Daffy Branch!

Finally they were all in. Pix fluttered up and locked the window. 'Right, let's go!' she whispered. 'And don't make any more noise than you can – *ack!*'

A glow-worm lantern had suddenly come on, flooding light into their faces. And holding it, standing not three inches away from them, was Mrs Lightwing!

The first-year head wore a dandelion-fluff dressing

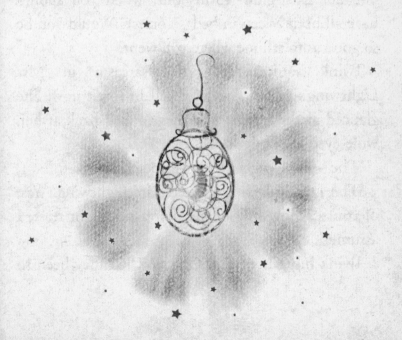

gown, her sky-blue hair tumbling loose across her shoulders. Her white wings tapped together as she stared hard at the girls. They shrank beneath her gaze.

'Would one of you care to explain why I was woken up by the sound of whispers outside the Great Branch, discussing various ways to break into it?' asked Mrs Lightwing.

Twink's wings felt like ice. 'I – we – we got stuck outside,' she blurted.

'I see,' Mrs Lightwing nodded. 'That would be outside, after glow-worms out, when you should have all been asleep in bed – correct? Would you be so good as to tell me where you went?'

Twink squirmed at the sarcasm in Mrs Lightwing's voice. They were all in for it now! She glanced at the others, and they looked back at her, wide-eyed. Nobody spoke.

'The – the Dingly Dell,' whispered Twink.

'The Dingly Dell,' repeated Mrs Lightwing. 'Yes, of course. How silly of me. For a midnight feast, I assume?'

Twink hung her head. Oh, *why* had they been so

daft as to leave the school! It had seemed like such a wonderful idea at the time.

'But, Mrs Lightwing, it's Twink's birthday!' Sooze stepped forward, her expression pleading. 'She was feeling sad about being away from her family, and we just wanted to make it special for her.'

There was a long pause. Twink held her breath.

'Get to bed, all of you,' snapped Mrs Lightwing finally. 'I'll deal with you in the morning!'

'Look!' hissed Sooze when they got back to Daffy Branch. 'It's just like I said – there she is, snoring away!'

Twink's heart sank. Sooze was right. Bimi was clearly asleep, her dark form gently rising and falling with every breath.

Sooze flitted across the room. 'And look at this,' she said, her voice shaking. She grabbed the petal from Bimi's cricket clock and held it up, clearly visible in the moonlight. *Seven o'clock* was written on it in Bimi's handwriting.

Twink stared at it in dismay.

Cricket clock

'Wasps,' whispered Pix. 'It looks like she really *did* leave us out there on purpose!'

Sili and Zena said nothing, looking grim. Twink bit her lip. *No!* she wanted to cry. But the petal spoke for itself.

Bimi stirred sleepily and rubbed her eyes. 'Are you all back already?' she murmured.

'Already!' burst out Sooze. 'It's after three o'clock – and thanks to *you*, we're all in trouble!'

'What?' Bimi's eyes widened. 'But – but I set my clock!'

'Yes, we see!' Sooze waved the petal in front of Bimi's face. 'Thanks a lot!'

Bimi turned on her glow-worm lamp and looked blankly at the writing on the petal. 'But I don't understand!' she cried. '*I* didn't write that – I set it for two o'clock, I really did.' She stared at them in confusion. 'How did you get back in?'

'When you didn't show up we had to sneak into the Great Branch, and we got caught by Mrs Lightwing,' said Pix flatly. 'But listen, everyone, we should go to bed now. We don't want to bring Mrs Lightwing up here and make it worse for ourselves!'

'What's all the noise?' demanded a grumpy voice. Across the branch, Mariella stirred. 'Some of us are trying to sleep!'

'Oh, be quiet!' snapped Sooze, turning on her. 'This has nothing to do with you!'

Lola had awakened too, and sat up. 'What's going on?' she squeaked.

'Something about Bimi setting her clock,' yawned Mariella, brushing back her silvery-green hair. 'Anyway, Bimi, you *did* set it – I heard you tell it seven o'clock as usual. So can we all go to sleep now?'

'There, *see*!' cried Sooze. 'Honestly, Bimi, I really wouldn't have thought it of you – even if you *don't* like me!'

'But I didn't! That's not what happened!' Bimi was near tears. 'Twink, *you* believe me, don't you?'

Twink hesitated. She didn't know what to think. The handwriting on the petal was Bimi's – and she knew how very angry and jealous her friend had been.

'I – I don't know,' she said miserably.

Bimi stared at Twink with wide, hurt eyes. 'Well – well, maybe I *did* do it in that case!' she said. 'And maybe you all deserved it!' She flopped on to her side with her back to them all, and pulled the covers up over her pointed ears.

'Oh!' breathed Sooze. 'See, she *did* do it!'

'GIRLS!' boomed a voice. Mrs Lightwing stood in the doorway, looking incensed.

'Oh, I knew it!' moaned Pix.

'WHICH PART OF *GO TO BED* DID YOU

NOT UNDERSTAND?'

The fairies scrambled for their beds, leaping into them without another word. Mrs Lightwing surveyed them coldly.

'I do not want to hear *another single sound* from this branch,' she said. 'And those of you who woke me up earlier, I'll see you in my office at eleven o'clock! Now, glow-worms out!'

The branch plunged into darkness. All was quiet – at first a stiff, angry silence, and then gradually the soft sounds of snores filled the air.

Even though she was exhausted, Twink lay awake for a long time, clutching the petal covers tightly around her. Tears stung at her eyes, and she wiped them away with a trembling hand.

How could Bimi have done such a thing to us? she thought wretchedly. *How?*

Chapter Five

'Our next three free afternoons gone!' moaned Sooze. 'And if *that* isn't bad enough, we have to clean all the windows in the school! It'll take us ages!'

'*Since you're so fascinated by windows.*' Zena made a face as she imitated the first-year head. They had just left Mrs Lightwing's office and were now flying glumly to their Dance lesson, her words still ringing in their ears.

Twink kept quiet. Secretly, she thought that Mrs Lightwing had been fair to them. Sneaking out at midnight was really very serious, even if they had only gone to the Dell.

'Anyway, the party was worth it, wasn't it?' Sooze bumped against Twink as they flew.

Twink's eyes shone as she nodded. 'It was the most wonderful party ever!' she said. And it had been . . . she just wished that Bimi hadn't played such an awful trick on them.

They landed in the circle of mushrooms where their Dance lessons were held. The rest of Daffy Branch was already there, waiting for them in the sunshine. Bimi looked away when she saw them, her mouth tight.

'What is this? You are all late!' cried Madame Brightfoot. Her vivid purple hair was piled atop her head, with loose wisps and curls falling down here and there.

'Sorry, Madame,' said Pix. 'We had to see Mrs Lightwing.'

'Ah!' Madame's long cobweb sleeves fluttered as she waved her arms about. 'You have all been bad fairies, no doubt! Bad, bad fairies who make my life a misery. Come now, get into a circle and join hands!'

The fairies fluttered into a circle, facing each other. Sili ended up beside Bimi, and she moved instantly, flying over to stand beside Twink instead. Bimi bit her lip, colouring up.

'What now? Why do you move?' snapped Madame.

Sili shrugged, not looking at Bimi. 'I just like it better over here.'

'I'll stand beside her,' said Sooze suddenly. Her eyes had a wicked gleam in them.

'Good girl! Come along, Sooze,' said Madame.

Sooze took Bimi's hand. Nobody else seemed to want to stand beside Bimi, but finally Lola was jostled into place beside her, and took her other hand with obvious reluctance. Bimi looked stiff and miserable. Glancing across the circle at her, Twink felt a pang.

But it's her own fault! she thought angrily. *She shouldn't have locked us out. She must have known how furious everyone would be with her!*

Madame flitted to the centre of the circle and clapped her hands. 'We will do the new dance I just taught you, where we make the wind blow! Ready? One, two, three, and we begin!'

Had Bimi locked them out, though? Twink's mind felt jumbled as they started to dance. Could she really have done such a thing? But if she hadn't, then what on earth had happened?

Slowly, Twink's thoughts faded as the dance continued. The magic was gathering around them:

tiny gold sparkles that glinted in the sun. She heard the wind coming, and felt it begin to rustle her long pink hair.

'Oh!' screeched Sooze, hopping on one foot. The magic vanished with little popping noises.

'What *now?*' demanded Madame, her hands on her hips.

'Bimi trod on my foot!' Sooze tried to take a step and grimaced, fluttering her wings. 'Ooh, it really hurts!'

'I did not!' cried Bimi.

Madame sighed and patted her purple hair into place. 'Bimi, try not to be so clumsy. Girls, get in a circle again. From the start!'

But the same thing happened over and over. No sooner had the magic started to gather than Sooze would stop with a yelp, insisting that Bimi had trod on her, or jostled her, or tripped her up.

'Oh!' cried Madame at last, throwing her arms into the air. 'I do not know what to think! Bimi, you are disrupting my class – you can leave, please!'

Bimi flew off without a word, her face on fire.

Twink watched her go and felt a lump in her throat as a few of the girls snickered.

I don't believe it, she thought suddenly. *It's not true. Bimi wouldn't do such a thing, no matter how angry she was!* Relief rushed through her. She was right, she just knew it.

But the wrong time had been written on Bimi's petal. With a worried frown, Twink looked across the circle as they started dancing again. Mariella was smirking broadly as she dipped and twirled, looking even more pleased with herself than usual.

A chill trembled across Twink's wings. Mariella! Of course!

'Don't be such a wasp brain,' said Sooze crossly. 'Bimi did it, all right. She practically admitted it, remember? Hold that bucket still.'

The girls were hovering high up in the air, washing the school's windows until they shone. Twink's arms ached as she held up the heavy walnut-bucket of soapy water for Sooze. Far below them, the flying field and pond looked tiny.

'But Sooze, Mariella could have done it,' insisted Twink. 'And you know it's the sort of thing she *would* do.'

'Could have and would have, maybe, but *didn't*.' Sooze flung her cotton wad back into the bucket with a splash. A robin sat on a branch beside them, watching with keen-eyed interest.

'Oh, flap off!' Sooze snapped at it. It huffed and flew away. 'Honestly, Twink, what's wrong with you?' she demanded. '*You* should be the one who's angriest about this. Bimi was supposed to be your best friend!'

Twink shook her head stubbornly as they flew to the next window. 'I know,' she said. 'But, Sooze, I just don't think she did it.'

'Well, you'll need proof to convince everyone,' said Sooze. She washed the window clean and made a face at her reflection. 'Because they're not going to believe you any more than I do!'

Sooze was right, realised Twink with a sinking heart. She needed proof. How, though? Mariella wasn't very likely to confess to her!

Lola, thought Twink suddenly. She tightened her grip on the bucket. That was it! If she could get the pale little fairy on her own, away from Mariella, she might be able to get her to talk.

But before Twink did anything else, she knew she had to apologise to Bimi. When the last window of the day had finally been cleaned, Twink sped off to find her friend.

Bimi didn't seem to be anywhere – not in the first-year Common Branch, or Daffy Branch, or anywhere outside. Finally she found the blue-haired fairy alone in the library, hovering high up beside the shelves. Twink took a deep breath and flew up next to her.

Bimi glanced at her and then quickly away again. She pulled out *Sparkle Bright: A True History of Fairy Dust* from the shelves and started flipping through it.

'What do you want?' she asked in a trembling voice.

'Oh, Bimi, I'm really sorry!' burst out Twink. 'I know you didn't lock us out on purpose. I've been

Library

such a wasp brain!'

Bimi stared down at her petal book, looking close to tears.

Twink touched her arm. 'Bimi, didn't you hear me? I'm so sorry! I know you would never do such a thing. I don't know how I ever thought you could have!'

'Well, *I* know!' cried Bimi. She shoved the petal book back into place. 'I've been just awful to you. Oh, Twink, I'm sorry too – I was so jealous of Sooze! It was just that she took over your party, and –' Bimi stopped, her face reddening.

'Took over my party?' repeated Twink in confusion. 'What do you mean? It was her idea, wasn't it?'

Bimi shook her head. 'No, it was mine,' she said tearfully. 'I didn't want to tell you – it seemed so petty to make a point of it! But it *was* my idea, only then Sooze thought of having it at the Dingly Dell, and she knew where to hide all the food and everything . . . by the time you found out, everyone had forgotten that I had anything to do with it.'

'Oh, Bimi!' breathed Twink. She didn't know what to say. How awful!

Bimi made a face. 'I know it was stupid of me to mind. But then Sooze gave you her present, and . . . well, just look.' Pulling a small package from the daisy bag she wore over one shoulder, she handed it to Twink.

'Oh,' breathed Twink. The present was beautifully wrapped in a yellow petal, with a burst of tiny golden flowers for a bow. She unwrapped it carefully.

'A snail-trail pen!' she exclaimed.

'I know, you already have one,' said Bimi sourly.

Twink shook her head. 'Not as nice as this one.'

Bimi stared at her. 'They're exactly the same!'

'They're *not*,' insisted Twink. '*You* gave me this one, and you're my best friend! It's the nicest present I've ever got.'

'Really?' whispered Bimi, her blue eyes wide and hopeful.

Twink nodded vehemently. 'I love it! I'll use it all the time, Bimi, really.'

For Twink

Bimi traced the title of one of the books with a finger. 'I – I couldn't believe it when Sooze gave you hers,' she admitted. 'It felt like she had ruined everything then. That's when I decided to not even *go* to the party. I'm really sorry, Twink.'

'That's OK,' said Twink. 'I suppose I'd have felt pretty awful too, in your boots! But, Bimi, you don't need to be jealous of Sooze. I like her, but it's not the same thing at all. *You're* my best friend!'

Bimi smiled, wiping her eyes. 'You're mine, too,' she said. 'I'll try not to be so jealous – I know it's daft of me.' The two fairies hugged in the air, their wings fluttering brightly.

'Now we just need to get the others to believe that you didn't do it!' said Twink as they pulled apart.

'Oh.' Bimi's face fell. 'They still think I did, then?'

Twink nodded grimly. 'Sooze says that they need proof. Bimi, you know who I think did it –'

'Mariella!' finished Bimi, her blue eyes flashing.

'Did you see her?' Twink clutched Bimi's arm as they hovered beside the shelf.

Bimi grimaced. 'No, but it *had* to be her. I've been thinking about it. She must have swapped my petal note for one with a different time, and copied my handwriting. It would have been the perfect way for her to get back at me, after I told everyone that I didn't like her in Flight class the other day!'

Twink nodded. 'I think so, too. But we have to get proof, so the others will believe us.'

Quickly, she told Bimi about her plan to get Lola on her own. 'We should pretend that we're still not talking,' she added. 'Or else Lola will know something's up, and she'll never tell me anything.'

'That's a good idea,' agreed Bimi. The swirls of silver and gold on her wings glinted as she fluttered thoughtfully. 'But, Twink, will you even be *able* to get Lola away from Mariella? Those two stick together like pine sap!'

Twink's jaw tightened. 'I'll try,' she said. 'If Lola is on her own for even just a second, I'll grab her!'

Chapter Six

But this turned out to be easier said than done. After a few days of trying to get Lola alone, Twink was ready to give up in despair. Just as Bimi had said, Lola stuck to Mariella's side like sticky sap. The two fairies seemed to do everything together – flying to class, going to the library, hovering together at break.

Finally Twink's luck turned in Flower Power class one afternoon, when Miss Petal looked over Mariella's homework with a frown. 'Mariella, this buttercup doesn't look at all well. Didn't you spend *any* time trying to heal it last night? Stay behind and see me after class, please!'

Twink exchanged a furtive glance with Bimi. This could be her chance!

Suddenly the magpie cry that signalled the end of class rang through the school. With a sulky look on her face, Mariella fluttered up to Miss Petal's desk.

The rest of the Daffy Branch fairies headed to their Creature Kindness class, halfway down the trunk. Twink's wings hummed as she raced to catch up with Lola. The pale fairy looked startled as Twink flew up beside her.

'Hi, Lola!' said Twink cheerfully.

'Um . . . hi.' Lola stared at Twink with distrust written plainly on her thin face.

'That was a great class, wasn't it?' continued Twink in a rush. 'I just love Miss Petal. She's so glimmery!'

Lola shrugged, still looking wary. 'She's OK.'

Twink glanced over her shoulder. No sign of Mariella yet, thank goodness! She lowered her voice. 'Listen, Lola, you know the other night, when –

when the rest of us had a midnight feast?'

Lola sniffed. 'You mean the one that Mariella and I weren't invited to!'

Oh, wasps, thought Twink. This wasn't going well at all. She took a deep breath. 'Yes, but – but I wanted to ask you something.'

A guilty look came over Lola's face. She hovered with her arms crossed over her chest. 'What?' she asked in a wavering voice.

Twink flew closer to her. 'Well – you know Bimi's cricket clock –'

'What about it?' demanded a voice. Mariella! The pointed-faced fairy flew up beside them. Her eyes narrowed as she looked from Lola to Twink and back again. Lola gulped.

'Nothing,' muttered Twink. 'I'm just . . . glad that we found out what Bimi's really like, that's all.'

'Yes, isn't she awful?' Mariella flipped back her silvery-green hair smugly. 'But then, *I* could have told you that ages ago.'

Oh! Twink's fists clenched as she watched Mariella link arms with Lola and fly away. That may have been her only chance, and she was no nearer to clearing Bimi's name than before.

She flew to one side as a chattering stream of Sixth Years streamed past, all looking very grown-up in their tight flower dresses. *I know Mariella did it,* she thought. *I just have to get her to admit it, somehow!* But how? Mariella would never confess on her own, and the only person she ever confided in was Lola.

Maybe that was it! Twink's heart thumped as an idea came to her. She flew on to class, deep in thought as she worked out a plan. Yes, that just might work!

'What's up, Opposite?' Sooze appeared beside her, pink wings fluttering as she did a quick somersault in the air. 'You look awfully serious!'

They had reached the Creature Kindness branch. 'Sooze, I've got to talk to you!' whispered Twink as they hovered beside the ledge.

'All right,' laughed Sooze. 'Talk away!'

'I know you don't believe me about Bimi,' said Twink in a low voice. 'But I think I have an idea that will prove it to you. Will you go along with it?'

Sooze was instantly serious . . . or at least as serious as Sooze ever was. She nodded. 'Of course I will. But I don't think you're going to prove anything to me, Twink. I really don't!'

Twink whispered quickly, outlining her plan. Just as she finished, Mr Woodleaf appeared in the doorway, his dark green wings flapping nervously. 'Girls? Hurry up, now – class is starting.'

Sooze winked at Twink. 'I'll do it!' she said.

Flying into the branch, the two girls took their mushroom seats. A sad-looking woodlouse sat on the table at the front, its grey antennae drooping.

'Now then,' said Mr Woodleaf, clearing his throat. 'Ahem . . . today we're going to discuss . . . ahem . . . how to cheer up woodlice.'

He spoke in a half-mumble, looking away from the girls. Twink sighed. She had been so looking forward to this class, but Mr Woodleaf seemed terrified of them!

Still, at least she had a chance to set her plan into action. Carefully tearing a petal from the notebook

Zena had given her, Twink wrote WE KNOW WHAT YOU DID TO BIMI on it. Folding the note into a tiny square, she passed it to Sooze when Mr Woodleaf wasn't looking.

Sooze sat beside Mariella. The pointed-faced fairy was leaning her head on her hand, her lacy green wings drooping with boredom.

Quick as a butterfly, Sooze tossed the note into Mariella's clover-leaf bag. Mariella yawned, not noticing a thing. A second later, Sooze was watching

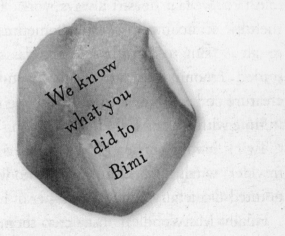

We know what you did to Bimi

with innocent interest as Mr Woodleaf explained how to cheer up a woodlouse by tickling its tummy.

'You see, you just . . . ah . . . turn it over on to its back, and give it a good tickle, like this . . .' The woodlouse looked aggrieved as Mr Woodleaf flipped it over and ran his fingers across its stomach.

The class stifled a giggle. The woodlouse looked almost ready to cry.

'Sir, maybe it's not ticklish!' said Pix. The class erupted into laughter. Even Mr Woodleaf managed a smile.

'Ah . . . well, it doesn't always work,' he admitted ruefully, scratching his head. 'Sometimes you have to, ah . . . sing to them . . .' To the class's delight, he started crooning loudly to the woodlouse. The creature perked up immediately, waving its antennae in time with the tune.

Twink hardly noticed. *When would Mariella find it?* Her wings felt clammy as she watched the pointed-faced fairy out of the corner of her eye.

Finally Mr Woodleaf instructed them all to take notes, and the class obediently reached into their

bags for pens and petals. As Mariella took out her petal pad, there was a tiny *plop*. The folded petal had fallen out of her bag on to the mossy carpet. Mariella gazed at it blankly, and then picked it up.

Twink's pulse pounded as she watched her unfold it. Mariella's face turned pale, and then bright red. Wings trembling with agitation, she glanced around the branch with narrowed eyes. Twink looked down, pretending to be involved in her note-taking.

Oh, please let it work, she thought, gripping her pen. They had break next. If Mariella stormed off in a huff with Lola, she and Sooze could follow her and try to overhear what they said.

The moment the magpie sounded at the end of class, Mariella leapt up from her mushroom. Sure enough, she grabbed Lola's arm and dragged the smaller fairy quickly from the branch.

'Hurry!' Twink hissed to Sooze. 'We have to follow them!'

The two girls grabbed their things and sped out of the branch. 'Which way did they go?' cried Twink, looking wildly around her. They wouldn't get

another chance if they lost them now!

'Down!' said Sooze, pointing. 'Look, they're heading for the library!'

Aiming themselves like arrows, the two fairies went into a steep dive, whistling through the air after Mariella and Lola. Sooze laughed. 'Even if this doesn't work, it's been glimmery fun so far!' she called.

Twink didn't answer. Nothing about it was fun, as far as she was concerned! She had to prove that Bimi was innocent, or the others would never want to be friends with her again.

Ahead of them, she saw Mariella and Lola swoop into the library. She grabbed Sooze's arm as they neared the library's ledge, slowing her down.

'We have to look casual,' she said. 'They can't notice us, no matter what!'

Mrs Stamen, the librarian, gave them a friendly smile as they flitted into the high-ceilinged room. 'Looking for something in particular, girls?'

'Er . . . no . . . just looking!' stammered Twink. They fluttered quickly away before Mrs Stamen could ask any more questions. Twink gazed around the library, her forehead creased. Where *were* they?

'Up there!' whispered Sooze, pointing. 'Look, they've gone behind that shelf near the ceiling!'

Glancing up, Twink saw the green flash of Mariella's wing as it disappeared behind one of the top shelves. 'Come on!' she said.

The two girls took off, weaving their way around the shelves as they flew higher and higher. The tall, narrow windows of the library flashed in the

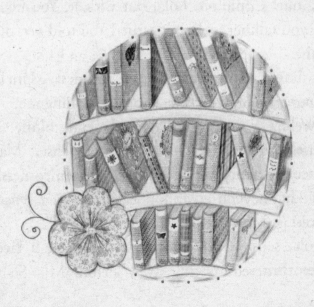

sunshine. Sooze gave an exaggerated shudder. 'I'm glad that Sili and Zena will be cleaning those, and not us!' she whispered.

'Listen!' hissed Twink, clutching her arm. They had come to the shelf on the other side of Mariella and Lola.

The two girls pressed their pointed ears against the bookcase. Mariella's voice came clearly, sharp and menacing.

'Well, if *you* didn't tell anyone, then how did they find out? Come on, Lola, out with it. You know I saw you talking to Twink earlier! You told *her*, didn't you?'

'I didn't!' whined Lola's voice. 'Honest, Mariella – I'd never tell on you. Ouch! Stop pinching me!'

'Well . . . I suppose it could be a bluff,' said Mariella after a short, considering pause. 'Maybe someone's hoping that I'll be scared into confessing. Ha! They're such a wet lot. I'm glad *you're* sensible, at least.'

Lola, sensible! Twink and Sooze made a face at each other.

'You don't think they really know anything, then?' asked Lola in her squeaky voice.

Twink's fingers tightened on the shelf as Mariella gave a sneering laugh. 'No, how could they? The only evidence is that petal I took from Bimi's bedside, and *that's* still safe in the pocket of my nightdress.'

'But – but shouldn't you throw it away?' quavered Lola.

'It's safe where it is. No one will find it there! Come on, let's get going – break's almost over with, and I want to get some sweet seeds from the tuck shop.'

There was a faint rustle of wings as they flew away. Twink and Sooze pressed against the book-case, ducking around the other side of it as Mariella and Lola appeared below them.

Sooze's face was stormy. 'That mean thing!' she burst out once they had gone. 'Twink, you were right. She did it, all right! Oh, just wait till I get my wings on her!'

Twink gripped her hand. 'Then you'll back me up

in front of the others?'

'Of course!' cried Sooze. Her pink wings fluttered heatedly. 'Oh, poor Bimi. We were horrible to her – me especially! We'll have to do something really nice to make it up to her.'

Sooze stopped suddenly. A mischievous smile grew across her face. 'Oh!' she said. 'That's it!'

'What?' demanded Twink.

Sooze grinned. 'I've just had the most glimmery idea ever, that's all! Come on, let's go and find the others before break's over with. I know exactly how we can get back at Mariella!'

Chapter Seven

Twink was certain that she'd be too excited to sleep that night, but she must have dropped off despite herself. The next thing she knew, Sooze was shaking her shoulder.

'Wake up, Opposite,' she hissed loudly. 'It's time!'

The fairies of Daffy Branch moved about in the moonlight, whispering and pulling on their dressing gowns. It was just like the night of Twink's birthday . . . except that this time, the whispers were quite a bit louder!

'Another midnight feast!' said Sili. 'This is going

to be such fun!'

'Yes, it's just the thing to make it up to Bimi for not believing her!' said Pix in a piercing whisper.

'I can hardly wait!' put in Bimi.

Twink could see her eyes sparkling in the moonlight. She felt a rush of gratitude towards Sooze. True to her word, Sooze had told everyone exactly what had really happened. They had all been as aghast and angry as she had been at Mariella's trick, and quick to offer apologies to Bimi – who had been only too glad to accept them!

A soft snore came from across the room. *Wasps!* thought Twink, biting her lip. Was Mariella *really* asleep . . . or just pretending? There was no way of knowing.

'Come on, everyone,' whispered Sooze loudly. She lit a tiny glow-worm lantern. 'Let's go – but *keep quiet*! We don't want that awful Mariella telling Mrs Lightwing what we're up to.'

The fairies took off into the moonlit trunk. Flying up to the first-year Common Branch, they went into a quick huddle.

'Zena, you wait out here and watch Daffy Branch,' hissed Sooze. 'Hide behind the ledge in case they sneak over here to make sure we're really having a party. The rest of us will go into the branch and act like we're having a good time.'

'We *are* having a good time!' put in Pix with a grin.

Leaving Zena, the fairies fluttered into the branch. 'Oh, it's so different in here at night!' breathed Twink. Her friends' faces looked ghostly, their wings gleaming as the light of the single lantern shone through them.

'Would you pass the sweet seeds, Twink?' asked Pix loudly.

'Of course!' Twink passed an imaginary plate to Pix. 'And have some of this sparkling dew, too!'

'Mmm, these pollen cakes are delicious!' said Bimi.

They chattered loudly about all the wonderful food they were eating. Sooze and Sili pretended to eat, solemnly chewing and drinking nothing at all. Twink bit her lip to keep from collapsing into

helpless giggles. If anyone could see them, they would think the Daffy Branch fairies had gone completely mad!

Suddenly Zena stuck her head around the door. 'Hurry!' she whispered. 'They've just been listening outside the ledge, and now they're zooming off towards Mrs Lightwing's branch!'

Quick as lightning, the fairies leapt up and ran from the Common Branch, launching into the air and plummeting downwards. In less than a minute, they were tucked up back in their beds in Daffy

Branch, with the lantern out and their dressing gowns put away.

'Remember, we've been asleep for ages!' whispered Sooze. The branch grew still, with only the soft sounds of pretend sleeping filling the air.

They heard Mrs Lightwing before they saw her. 'What on *earth* is the meaning of this, Mariella? You wake me up in the middle of the night to tell me that the others are having a feast in the Common Branch, and no one is there!'

'But they *were* there!' protested Mariella. She sounded furious, and the fairies had to burrow their faces in their pillows to keep from laughing. 'They must have gone somewhere else!'

'They were there, really they were!' echoed Lola's squeaky voice. 'They had all sorts of food, and drink, and –'

'Glow-worms on!' barked Mrs Lightwing. Suddenly Daffodil Branch was flooded with light. There was a pause.

Opening her eyes the tiniest crack, Twink saw the first-year head standing in the doorway with her hands on her hips. Mariella and Lola looked stunned, with their mouths hanging open and rather silly expressions on their faces.

'Well?' demanded Mrs Lightwing. 'What do you have to say for yourself, Mariella?'

'I – I – it's a trick!' stammered Mariella. 'They were all having a feast, they really were –'

Mrs Lightwing tapped her wings together and scowled at the pointed-faced fairy.

'Well, if they *have* been playing a trick on you, I suspect they had good reason. We don't like tell-tales here at Glitterwings, Mariella – bear that in mind next time! Meanwhile, for waking me up for no good reason, you and Lola will both finish the window-washing that the others have been doing. I believe that they've only got about halfway through, so you'll have plenty to keep you busy!'

'But that's not *fair*!' burst out Mariella. 'They were –'

'Would you like to wash *all* the windows?' snapped Mrs Lightwing. Mariella fell into a fuming silence.

'No, I thought not!' said Mrs Lightwing. 'Now, go to bed. Glow-worms off!'

She took off from the ledge. No one said a word until they were quite sure she was gone, and then Pix stirred drowsily, sitting up in bed and rubbing her eyes.

'What's going on?' she murmured. 'What was all that noise?'

'You mean things!' Mariella stamped her foot. 'You *were* having a feast, you were!'

Twink lit a lantern and jumped out of bed. 'We *weren't*,' she said fiercely. 'We were paying you back for what you did to Bimi, that's all – and you deserved every bit of it. Show her, Sooze!'

'With pleasure!' Sooze leapt up and flitted over to Mariella. 'Come on,' she said, holding out her hand. 'Let's see what you've got in the pocket of your nightdress!'

Mariella's cheeks burned. She tossed her silvery-green hair. 'I don't know what you mean. I don't have anything in my pocket!'

'Then turn it inside out, and let us see for

ourselves,' demanded Sooze, stepping forward.

Mariella gulped and backed away. 'I won't! Why should I?'

'I'll help you, then!' Quick as a bee-sting, Sooze lunged forward. Darting her hand into Mariella's pocket, she pulled out a crumpled bit of petal.

'Look, everyone,' she said, holding it up. 'It's just like we told you! Bimi wrote *two o'clock* on it, and Mariella swapped it for another one once Bimi fell asleep!'

The fairies stared stonily at the scrap of petal. Seeing it for themselves made Mariella's trick seem even worse.

'You should be ashamed of yourself, you horrid thing,' said Zena coldly. 'You knew we'd all blame Bimi!'

'I – I didn't mean anything *really* bad by it,' muttered Mariella. She had backed up almost against the wall by now, and looked quite sick. 'It was just meant to be a joke. Wasn't it, Lola?'

The thin little fairy nodded vigorously. 'Of course! Mariella wouldn't do anything bad. It was

just a bit of fun.'

'Yes, great fun!' cried Twink. Her lavender wings trembled. 'Poor Bimi had to put up with everyone turning against her, and we lost three free afternoons washing windows! Well, you got what you deserve, Mariella.'

'And you too, Lola,' added Pix sternly. 'You should choose your friends better!' She turned to Bimi, who had stood pale and quiet throughout all of this. 'Bimi, I know we all said sorry to you before, but I want to say it again. We should have known that you'd never do such a thing!'

The others clustered around Bimi, echoing agreement. Sooze fluttered over and looked Bimi squarely in the eye. 'I'm sorry, too,' she said. 'I was the worst of anyone. Will you forgive me, Bimi?'

Bimi nodded. 'Of course! And, Sooze, I – well – maybe I was wrong about you,' she said in a rush. 'I'm sorry, too.'

Happiness burst through Twink as Sooze and Bimi hugged, their wings fluttering. Oh, how perfectly glimmery! Her two friends, friends at last!

'But we still haven't decided what to do about Mariella and her little insect friend,' said Sooze grimly as she and Bimi pulled apart. She gave the two fairies a hard look.

'What do you mean?' cried Mariella in alarm. She shrank against the wall. 'I've already been given my punishment.'

'Not by *us*, you haven't,' said Zena. 'And we're the ones who have to live with you!'

'I think Bimi should decide what to do,' said Twink. She stepped close to her friend and squeezed her hand encouragingly.

'Yes, that's fair,' said Pix. 'She was the one most hurt by Mariella. What do you think, Bimi? What should we do about them?'

Bimi hesitated, biting her lip. 'Well,' she said slowly, '. . . since Mariella and Lola seem to dislike us so much . . . maybe we should do them a favour and stop talking to them for a while.'

'Perfect!' said Pix. She turned towards Mariella and Lola, who stood huddled together, wings touching.

'From this moment on, no fairy in Daffy Branch will say a word to either of you,' said Pix firmly. 'Not until we decide that you've learned your lesson. And we'll make sure that the rest of the first year follows suit!'

'But I didn't mean it!' Mariella looked close to tears. 'It was only a joke, that's all! Can't you take a joke?'

Sooze looked blankly around the branch. 'Did anyone hear anything?'

The other fairies chorused that they hadn't.

'Come on, everyone, let's go to bed.' Pix's yellow wings fluttered as she stifled a yawn. 'We've got to get up in the morning, and we're going to be tired enough as it is.'

'Oh, Twink, do you think I was too hard on them?' whispered Bimi as they snuggled down against the soft moss of their beds. 'I feel really sorry for them now!'

Twink looked across the branch. Mariella lay in a miserable huddle with her covers up over her ears. Lola was sobbing into her pillow. Despite herself, Twink felt a twinge of sympathy.

'I know,' she said softly. 'But they brought it on themselves, Bimi – they have to learn their lesson, or else they'll just keep on being horrid.' She smiled suddenly. 'Besides, at least now we'll get some peace and quiet for a while!'

The summer term continued in a haze of glorious sunshine and long days. The fairies tried hard to concentrate on their classes, but it was difficult when all they wanted to do was flit about outside, enjoying the sun on their wings. At least, thought Twink, they had the spectacle of Mariella and Lola washing windows to keep them amused!

At dinner a few weeks later, Miss Shimmery called for attention.

'You may have noticed how lovely and shiny all of our school windows are.' She motioned towards the windows of the Great Branch, which sparkled in the late-afternoon sun. 'Well, we have some of our first-year students to thank for that!'

Miss Shimmery's rainbow wings glimmered as she smiled down at the Daffodil Branch table. 'They were having a hard time settling down this term, so we found them some extra work, just as promised. But let's give them a round of applause, shall we? They've really done a wonderful job!'

The Branch burst into applause. The Daffodil Branch fairies grinned at each other – apart from Mariella and Lola, who sat glumly, not looking pleased at all. Miss Shimmery returned to her table and the students began to eat, chatting and laughing.

'I suppose we can start talking to those two again now,' said Pix, glancing at Mariella and Lola. 'But you'd both better watch it – we won't put up with any more mean tricks like that.'

Mariella nodded sullenly. 'Yes, all right. And – and I'm sorry, Bimi,' she added, not looking the blue-haired fairy in the eye. Twink didn't think she really sounded sorry . . . though maybe it was a start!

Bimi looked doubtful too, but she nodded. 'That's all right, Mariella. I know you won't do anything like that again.'

Sooze nudged Twink with her wing. 'You know, I think we should do something to celebrate all those windows being cleaned.' Her violet eyes were round and innocent. 'How about a midnight feast?'

The rest of the table groaned loudly. 'No, no midnight feasts for a while!' said Twink with an exaggerated shudder. 'I think we've had enough excitement this term!'

'I know *I* have,' said Bimi with a grin.

Sooze laughed. 'You can never have enough excitement!'

Twink helped herself to another seed cake, chewing happily as the table buzzed with conversation around her. The party at the Dingly Dell had been glimmery – the most magical, wonderful time ever. They'd go back there again one day, she knew.

Twink looked at Bimi, and the two fairies smiled at each other. And next time, thought Twink, she'd make sure that her best friend was right there with her!

The End

Read on
for the glimmery
beginning of Twink's
next adventure

Friends Forever

'Now then, class.' Madame Brightfoot hovered in front of the Daffodil Branch fairies and patted her bright purple hair into place. 'Today we learn a new dance! Today, we learn how to find creatures in distress.'

Twink Flutterby shot an excited glance at Bimi, her best friend. 'Glimmery!' she whispered. It was a fairy's duty to take care of nature, but as first-year students, Twink and her friends hadn't had many chances to do this yet.

Bimi's dark blue eyes shone. 'I wonder if we'll actually get to help something?'

A thrill rippled through Twink's wings. 'Oh, I hope so! I'd love to tell my parents that.' Twink's parents were both Fairy Medics, and it was Twink's dearest wish to follow in their wing strokes some day.

'Form a circle!' called Madame, waving her slender arms. 'Quick, quick!'

Madame Brightfoot's Dance class was held in an enchanted ring of mushrooms near the wood. Behind them, the great oak tree that housed Glitterwings Academy was ablaze with autumn, its leaves on fire with red and gold and orange. Hundreds of tiny windows wound their way up the tree's trunk, and the grand double doors at its base looked shiny and welcoming.

The Daffodil Branch fairies stood in a circle, holding hands.

'Flower position!' Madame shot up into the air, her spiderweb dress shimmering.

The fairies opened their wings so that the very

tips of them touched. Twink squeezed Bimi's hand. Across the circle, she saw her friend Sooze bouncing on her toes, and she grinned. Sooze loved trying anything new!

Clasping her hands, Madame slowly sank back down to earth. Her voice was low and solemn. 'Now, this dance is very different from the others you've learned. It is a most serious dance.'

She looked around the circle, her expression grave. Twink swallowed. The class grew very still as they all gazed back at her.

Finally Madame nodded. 'Close your eyes, everyone.'

Twink shut her eyes, listening closely as Madame went on.

'You must all concentrate together on hearing any nearby creatures in distress – and with the magic of the dance, you'll be able to understand what they're telling you if they respond. Now . . . two skips left, two skips right, dip, twirl, and rise.'

They began to dance. The air felt alive with sparkles as the magic gathered.

'Now rise!' said Madame's voice.

The fairies lifted into the air, their wings humming softly. 'Again!' directed Madame. 'Concentrate!'

Does anything need our help? thought Twink as her feet moved in the air.

They repeated the dance over and over. The magic swelled until it felt like a thousand tiny bubbles swirling around them – and still the dance went on. Wasn't anything going to happen?

Are there any creatures that need our help? thought Twink again, concentrating harder than ever. *We want to help you!*

Suddenly she heard it: a small, frightened voice inside her head. *Yes!* it called. *Help me, please!* Twink gasped, and almost dropped Bimi's hand.

Where are you? she thought eagerly.

The little voice came again. *In the wood! Please help me!*

We will! thought Twink as loudly as she could. *Don't worry, we're coming!*

Collect the series and discover even more sparkly
stories full of friendship, adventure and fairy fun!

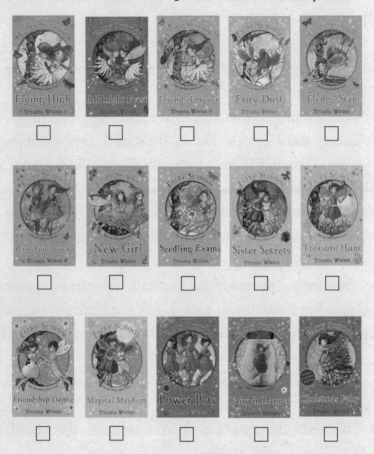

Flying High	Midnight Feast	Friends Forever	Fairy Dust	Pledge Star
☐	☐	☐	☐	☐

Term-Time Trouble	New Girl	Seedling Exams	Sister Secrets	Treasure Hunt
☐	☐	☐	☐	☐

Friendship Dance	Magical Mayhem	Power Play	Fairy in Danger	Christmas Fairy
☐	☐	☐	☐	☐

Visit **www.fairyschoolbooks.co.uk** to meet Twink and
all her fantastic fairy friends!